D1179746

Short Tales
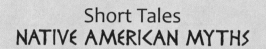
NATIVE AMERICAN MYTHS

SKY WOMAN AND THE BIG TURTLE

AN IROQUOIS CREATION MYTH

Adapted by Anita Yasuda
Illustrated by Mark Pennington

magic
wagon

visit us at www.abdopublishing.com

Published by Magic Wagon, a division of the ABDO Group, PO Box 398166, Minneapolis, MN 55439. Copyright © 2013 by Abdo Consulting Group, Inc. International copyrights reserved in all countries. All rights reserved. No part of this book may be reproduced in any form without written permission from the publisher.

Short Tales™ is a trademark and logo of Magic Wagon.

Printed in the United States of America, North Mankato, Minnesota.
052012
092012

 THIS BOOK CONTAINS AT LEAST 10% RECYCLED MATERIALS.

Adapted text by Anita Yasuda
Illustrations by Mark Pennington
Edited by Rebecca Felix
Series design by Craig Hinton

Design elements: Diana Walters/iStockphoto

Library of Congress Cataloging-in-Publication Data
Yasuda, Anita.
  Sky woman and the big turtle : an Iroquois creation myth / by Anita Yasuda ; illustrated by Mark Pennington.
     p. cm. -- (Short tales native American myths)
  ISBN 978-1-61641-882-3
  1. Iroquois Indians--Folklore. 2. Iroquois mythology. I. Pennington, Mark, 1959- ill. II. Title.
  E99.I7Y28 2012
  299.7'855024--dc23
                      2012004695

MYTHICAL CHARACTERS

LITTLE TURTLE

Creates the sun
and the moon

TOAD

Gathers the earth that
grows into North America

BIG TURTLE

A creature on whose back
North America rests

SKY WOMAN

A woman who fell from
the sky

EVIL-SPIRITED TWIN

Creator of all that is bad

GOOD-SPIRITED TWIN

Creator of all that is good

INTRODUCTION

This legend comes from the Iroquois people. The Iroquois are also known as the Haudenosaunee or "People of the Longhouse." The Iroquois originally lived in the area now known as New York. Iroquois legends are an important way for customs and histories to be passed down through the generations. The Iroquois people would gather in longhouses and listen as elders told stories.

Sky Woman and the Big Turtle shows the Iroquois's respect for animals and their important role in creating North America. This legend is just one version of the Iroquois creation story. It serves as a reminder of people's connection to the world around them. The story teaches the audience that he or she should take care of Earth.

Long ago, the first people lived in the sky, as there was no Earth.

The Sky People were happy and content. No one was ever sad and no one ever died.

One day, the Sky Chief's daughter became ill. No one knew how to cure her. The Sky People had never seen a sick person before. They could only shake their heads.

"I will ask the elder," the Sky Chief said.

6

"You must dig up a tree and place your daughter by its hole," the elder said.

The Sky People dug and dug. It seemed as if the task would never end.

Suddenly, the tree fell through the hole. The Sky People scattered as the tree fell, but Sky Woman could not run away. Her hair became entangled in the branches, pulling her toward the water below.

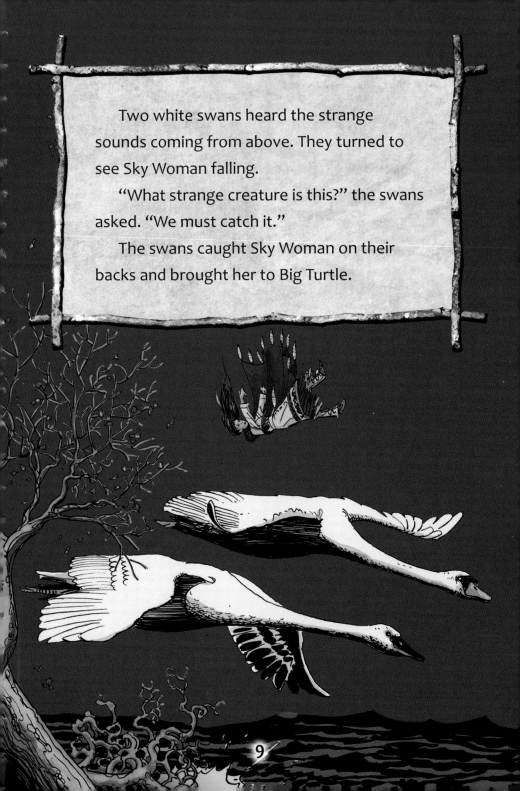

Two white swans heard the strange sounds coming from above. They turned to see Sky Woman falling.

"What strange creature is this?" the swans asked. "We must catch it."

The swans caught Sky Woman on their backs and brought her to Big Turtle.

Big Turtle gathered all the animals.
"This Sky Woman is very special," Big
Turtle said. "We must make her a home."
"How can we do that?" the animals asked.

"You must find the fallen tree with its earth-covered roots," Big Turtle said.

Only then, Big Turtle explained, could they make Sky Woman a home.

"We can show you where the tree landed," said the swans.
They led the animals to the spot.

"Stand back," Otter said. "I will go first."

And Otter dove into the water. Search as he might, Otter could not find the tree.

"I will go next," Muskrat said.

And Muskrat dove into the water. Search as he might, Muskrat could not find the tree.

"Let me try," Beaver said.

And Beaver dove into the water. Search as he might, Beaver could not find the tree either.

Then a small voice spoke up and said, "I can do it."

Surprised, the animals turned and saw that it was Toad.

"A toad as small as you?" the animals asked, laughing. "What could you possibly do?"

"Just watch me," Toad said. And she dove into the water.

Toad was gone a very long time. The other animals began to worry. Suddenly, she popped to the surface. Toad had a bit of earth in her mouth!

"She did it!" the animals cried.

Exhausted, Toad spit the earth onto the back of Big Turtle. The earth was magical. It grew into a magnificent island. When it was large enough for Sky Woman, the swans placed her on it.

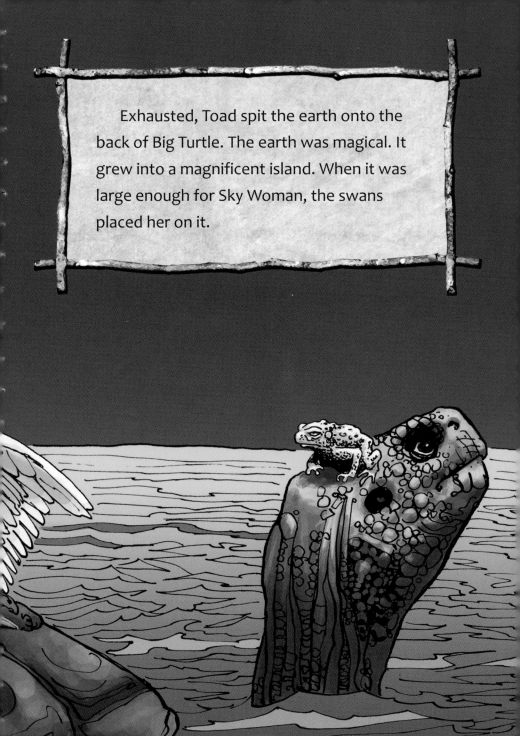

The swans swam around the island, encouraging it to grow more. The island grew and grew until it became as large as North America.

But the land was dark. Big Turtle and the other animals came up with a plan.

"We must put a light in the sky," the animals said.

Little Turtle stepped forward. "I can do it," she said.

20

And Little Turtle, with the help of the other animals, climbed into the sky. From a great black cloud, she gathered lightning.

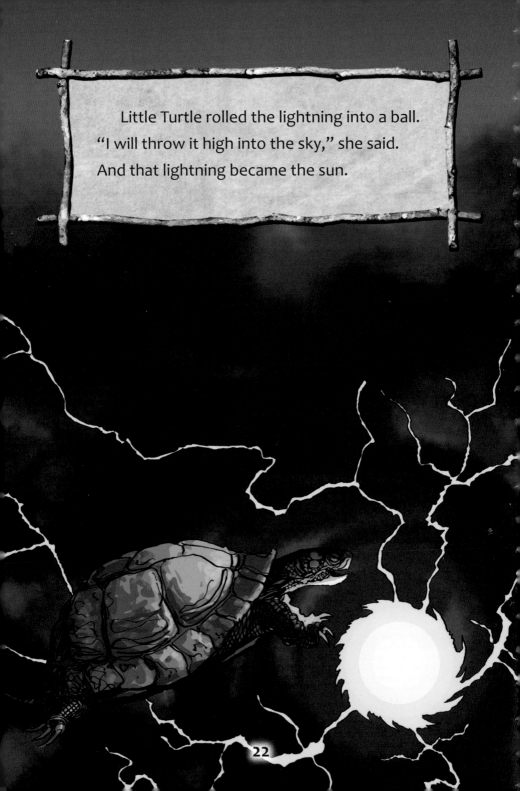

Little Turtle rolled the lightning into a ball. "I will throw it high into the sky," she said. And that lightning became the sun.

Little Turtle gathered more lightning into a ball.

"I will throw this into the sky, too," she said.

And that lightning became the moon.

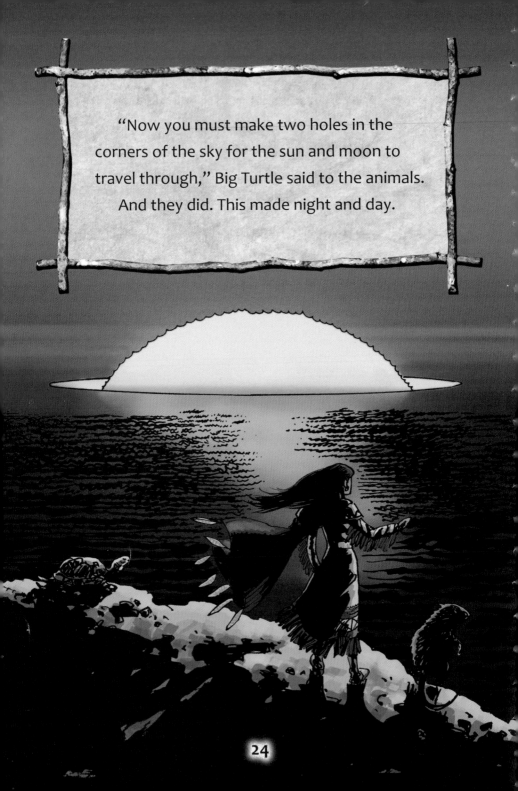

"Now you must make two holes in the corners of the sky for the sun and moon to travel through," Big Turtle said to the animals. And they did. This made night and day.

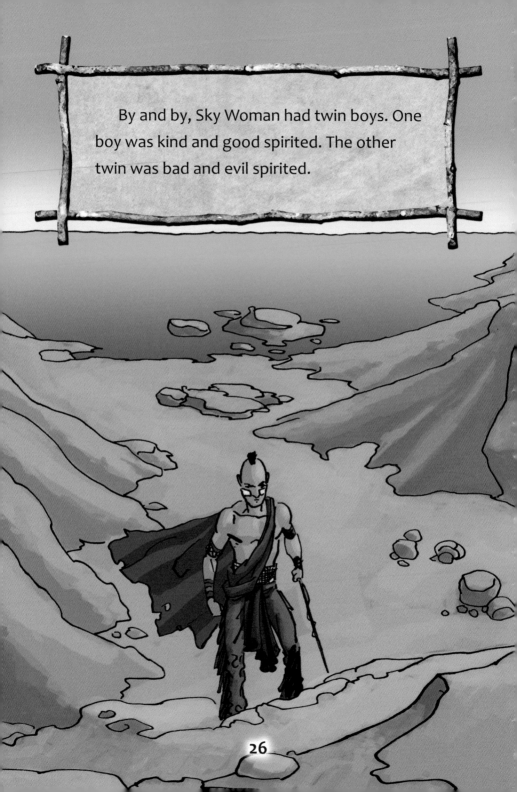

By and by, Sky Woman had twin boys. One boy was kind and good spirited. The other twin was bad and evil spirited.

The twin boys filled the land with their creations.

"I will create only good things," said the good-spirited twin. He made animals and plants people would find useful.

"I will create only bad things," said the evil-spirited twin. He put rapids and boulders in rivers and thorns on bushes.

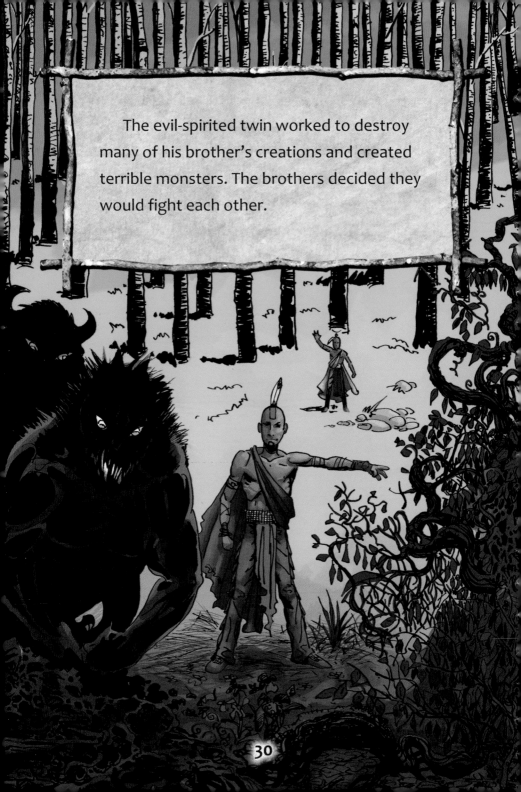

The evil-spirited twin worked to destroy many of his brother's creations and created terrible monsters. The brothers decided they would fight each other.

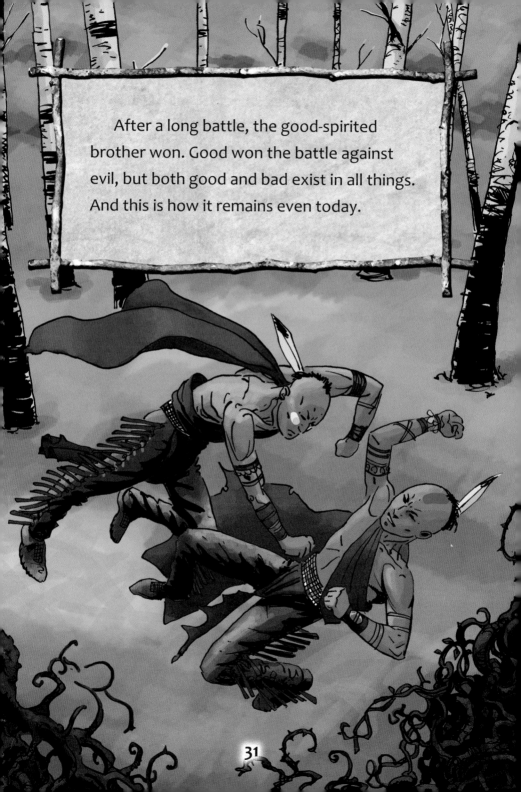

After a long battle, the good-spirited brother won. Good won the battle against evil, but both good and bad exist in all things. And this is how it remains even today.

People were then created to live on the land. And to this day, Big Turtle still carries the land on his back. Sometimes he stretches out his legs, causing the earth to tremble.